T0150947

MISTATIM / INSTANT

ALSO BY ERIN SHIELDS

If We Were Birds
Paradise Lost
Soliciting Temptation

MISTATIM

CONCEPT BY SANDRA LARONDE

—

INSTANT

ERIN SHIELDS

PLAYWRIGHTS CANADA PRESS
TORONTO

For professional or amateur production rights, please contact:
Ian Arnold at Catalyst TCM
312-100 Broadview Ave., Toronto, ON M4M 3H3
416.568.8673 :: ian@catalysttcm.com

LIBRARY AND ARCHIVES CANADA CATALOGUING IN PUBLICATION
Shields, Erin
[Plays. Selections]
      Mistatim ; Instant / by Erin Shields ; concept for Mistatim by Sandra Laronde.

Plays.
Issued in print and electronic formats.
ISBN 978-1-77091-929-7 (softcover).--ISBN 978-1-77091-930-3 (PDF).--
ISBN 978-1-77091-931-0 (EPUB).--ISBN 978-1-77091-932-7 (Kindle)

      I. Laronde, Sandra II. Shields, Erin. Mistatim. III. Shields, Erin.
Instant. IV. Title.

PS8637.H497A6 2018   jC812'.6   C2018-905798-X
                                                  C2018-905799-8

Playwrights Canada Press acknowledges that we operate on land which, for thousands of years, has been the traditional territories of the Mississaugas of the New Credit, the Huron-Wendat, Anishinaabe, Métis and Haudenosaunee peoples. Today, this meeting place is home to many Indigenous peoples from across Turtle Island and we are grateful to have the opportunity to work and play here.

We acknowledge the financial support of the Canada Council for the Arts—which last year invested $153 million to bring the arts to Canadians throughout the country—the Ontario Arts Council (OAC), the Ontario Media Development Corporation and the Government of Canada for our publishing activities.

Canada Council   Conseil des arts
for the Arts   du Canada

ONTARIO ARTS COUNCIL
CONSEIL DES ARTS DE L'ONTARIO
an Ontario government agency
un organisme du gouvernement de l'Ontario

Canadä

Ontario
Ontario Media Development
Corporation

For my friend, Joc Palm

FOREWORD
BY STEPHEN COLELLA

Erin Shields's work with Sandra Laronde at Red Sky Performance and Dean Fleming at Geordie Theatre led to the creation of two individually compelling pieces of work for young audiences: *Mistatim* and *Instant*. It was with great pleasure that we were able to program the presentation of both at Young People's Theatre (YPT). Each season at YPT is programmed around a theme or idea. *Mistatim* appeared in our fiftieth anniversary season, which was built upon YPT founder Susan Rubes's belief that "only the best is good enough for children." *Instant* played two seasons later under the theme "finding yourself." I think these plays could have appeared interchangeably in either season as these two notions could hold true for both.

On the surface these two stories seem to have very little in common. In one, two people on traditional Cree territory attempt to save a horse. In the other, three people look to the Internet, and the fame that it brings, as a way to solve their individual problems.

The link between these plays is found not on the stage or page but in the audience who attends. The young protagonists in these pieces grapple with complex and challenging issues in their lives—problems of their own making as well as those visited upon them by the adults in their lives. By presenting these topics realistically and authentically through the life of her characters, Erin shows respect not just to the characters and those who have faced similar circumstances, but also to young people who crave acknowledgement that they are capable of examining and responding to these experiences. It is through the thoughtful and nuanced presentation of truth that Erin's writing asks permission from a young audience for their trust—and in doing so receives their complete engagement.

These plays are honest about the world. At the same time they are careful not to ignore that hope is central to the lives of these young people. Hope's glow may be dull at the start of these stories, or grow dim as we move through them . . . but the light is never extinguished. Whether it is Calvin's belief that he can make his father listen in *Mistatim* or Meredith finding the courage to risk embarrassment and share her voice with the world in *Instant*, the audience knows that there is hope for a better way forward. Change must be earned, it may come at a cost, and it will not erase the past, but it is a road that can be walked. Erin's plays for young audiences never fail to fulfill that responsibility: holding up the light in the dark so that we can see hope.

Stephen Colella is Associate Artistic Director and Dramaturg at Young People's Theatre. His work there includes direction and dramaturgy for *Selfie* (Dora Award, Outstanding TYA Play and PGC TYA Award); dramaturgy for over fifteen world premieres, including *Hana's Suitcase*, *i think i can* (Dora Award, Outstanding New Musical), *Scarberia*, *Sultans of the Street* (Dora Award, Outstanding TYA Play) and *Minotaur* (YPT/Polka Theatre/Theatr Clwyd); and co-adapting *Love You Forever . . . And More Munsch* (Dora Award/Canada Council Theatre for Young Audiences Prize) and *Munschtime!*. Other work includes dramaturgy for Alameda Theatre, Marionetas de la Esquina/Kennedy Center, fu-Gen Theatre and the Paprika Festival. He is currently President of ASSITEJ Canada and has served on the board of the Literary Managers and Dramaturgs of the Americas and LMDA Canada.

MISTATIM
BY ERIN SHIELDS

CONCEPT BY SANDRA LARONDE
PLAINS CREE TRANSLATION BY
OKIYSIKAW TYRONE TOOTOOSIS

For those who are sharing their stories.
And those who are listening.

ACKNOWLEDGEMENTS

Thank you to Sandra Laronde and Red Sky Performance for inviting me to participate in this project. Thank you to all of the artists involved in the original production for contributing to the development of the script. Thank you to artists Alan Dilworth, Jakob Ehman, Bahareh Yaraghi and Carlos Rivera for workshopping an early draft. Thank you to Andrea Donaldson for directing such a beautiful piece. A special thank you to Okiysikaw Tyrone Tootoosis for his translations of the text into Plains Cree. And to Winona Wheeler for her generous help in editing and approving these translations.

Mistatim was commissioned and produced by Red Sky Performance in 2015 under Executive and Artistic Director Sandra Laronde. Based in Toronto, Red Sky Performance is a leading company of contemporary Indigenous performance in Canada and worldwide. *Mistatim* has toured nationally and internationally since 2015 with the following cast and creative team:

Mistatim: Carlos Rivera
Speck: Sera-Lys McArthur
Calvin: Brendan McMurtry-Howlett

Concept, Dramaturgy, Co-choreography: Sandra Laronde
Direction: Andrea Donaldson
Co-choreography: Carlos Rivera
Composer: Rick Sacks
Associate Sound Designer: Marc Meriläinen
Set and Video Designer: Andy Moro
Costume Designers: Elaine Redding and Charlene Seniuk
Cree Translator and Coach/Advisor: Okiysikaw Tyrone Tootoosis
Mask Design and Build: Karen Rodd
Mask Coach: Sonia Norris
Fight Director: Daniel Levinson

Other cast members on various durations of the tour included: Samantha Brown, Dakota Hebert, Dustin Luck, Jesse LaVercombe and Falciony Patiño Cruz.

CHARACTERS

Speck: eleven-year-old girl, Plains Cree
Calvin: eleven-year-old boy, non-Aboriginal Canadian
Mistatim (Bruiser): a wild horse owned by Calvin's family

SET

The only set piece is a fence that separates Calvin's ranch from Speck's reserve. The fence is moved throughout the play to offer different perspectives of the same place. It should not seem as though the fence is literally moving, but that the vantage point of the same place is changing.

PROJECTION

Projections appear on the back wall of the playing space throughout the play. When projections are not indicated in the script, a clear blue prairie sky is projected.

LANGUAGE

Plains Cree is spoken by Mistatim and Speck, and is included in the play as phonetic transcription. The English translation follows the Cree text in brackets. It should not be spoken.

SCENE 1

Lights slowly rise on a field in the middle of the prairies.
A projection on the back wall shows a bright blue endless sky.

MISTATIM charges onto the stage.
He is in the field at daybreak.
He dances the dance of the wild horse.
He moves with reckless abandon.
He is free.

SPECK enters and watches the horse from across the fence.
She approaches slowly, mirroring his movements.
She is connected to MISTATIM.
She is drawn to him.
He senses her presence.

MISTATIM   *(voice-over)* Mistatim. Mistatim. Mistatim.

SCENE 2

> CALVIN *enters cracking his whip.*
> SPECK *hides.*
> CALVIN *whips* MISTATIM.

SPECK   Stop!

CALVIN   *(jumping back)* Whoa!

SPECK   You're hurting him.

CALVIN   No I'm not.

SPECK   He's bleeding.

CALVIN   He barely feels it.

SPECK   He's hurt.

CALVIN   This is how you break a horse.

SPECK   He's scared.

CALVIN   He's supposed to be.

SPECK   Why?

CALVIN   So he'll know I'm in charge and he'll do what I say. That's the way it's done.

SPECK   Says who?

CALVIN   My dad.

SPECK   Then your dad doesn't know anything about horses.

CALVIN   We've got about eighty horses we breed and sell and rent out to farmers all over so I think my dad knows a thing or two about horses.

SPECK   Then why is this horse still wild?

CALVIN   His mother died before we got him so he never learned how to act with horses or people.

SPECK   And you think whipping him will change all that?

CALVIN   Who are you anyway?

SPECK   Speck.

CALVIN   Speck?

SPECK   They call me Speck because that's what my grandmother said when she saw me. "She's nothing but a speck," she said, and everyone agreed, so they called me Speck from the day I was born.

CALVIN   Don't you have a real name?

SPECK   Of course I have a real name.

CALVIN   What is it?

SPECK   I don't know.

CALVIN   You don't even know your name?

SPECK   Why do you care anyway?

CALVIN   I don't. It's just weird.

SPECK   Yah? What's yours?

CALVIN   Calvin.

SPECK   Calvin?!

CALVIN   What?

SPECK   And you're laughing at my name?

CALVIN   What's wrong with Calvin? Calvin's just normal.

SPECK   And that's what you want?

CALVIN   Huh?

SPECK   To be normal?

    Beat.

CALVIN   You live over there?

SPECK   Yah.

CALVIN   Why haven't I seen you before?

SPECK   I didn't want you to see me before.

CALVIN   What's that supposed to mean?

SPECK   I'm good at knowing when to run.

CALVIN   You don't go to my school.

SPECK   No.

CALVIN   Don't you go to school?

SPECK   What, you think because I'm Indian I don't go to school?

CALVIN   No . . . I just . . . my school's the only school.

SPECK   No it's not. There's a school on my reserve.*

CALVIN   But kids from the reserve go to my school.

SPECK   Not all of them.

CALVIN   I didn't know that.

SPECK   You don't know much, do you?

CALVIN   I know you shouldn't say Indian.

SPECK   Why not?

CALVIN   You should say First Nations or Aboriginal.**

SPECK   I can say whatever I want to say.

CALVIN   It's racist.

SPECK   You can't be racist about yourself.

> *Beat.*

---

* For an American production, replace "reserve" with "reservation."

** For an American production, replace with, "You should say Native American or Native American Indian."

CALVIN   I gotta go for breakfast.

>   *Beat.*

Come on, Bruiser.

>   *CALVIN uncoils the whip.*

Come on.

>   *He whips the horse.*
>   *MISTATIM rears.*

Come on.

>   *He whips him again.*

Come on.

>   *He starts to whip him again but MISTATIM charges.*
>   *MISTATIM pauses then retreats.*

SPECK   He's wild because he wants to be wild. No whip is going to change that.

CALVIN   *(to MISTATIM)* Fine! Stay here then!

>   *CALVIN stomps off.*
>   *MISTATIM is agitated from the whip.*
>   *SPECK locks eyes with him.*
>   *They breathe together.*
>   *MISTATIM suddenly bolts away.*
>   *Lighting shift.*

SCENE 3

SPECK is flooded with memory.
She dreams.
A projection of hands appears behind her:
  • *a child holds the hand of an adult*
  • *the hands are pulled apart*
  • *the sequence replays at different speeds*
SPECK examines her hands as the images play and
replay.
MISTATIM whinnies loudly as if to wake SPECK.
Lighting shift.

SCENE 4

Lights up on the fence.
SPECK's side is downstage.
Names are carved into the fence.
SPECK sits and plays a throwing game with small
rocks.
MISTATIM grazes upstage of the fence.

CALVIN enters, whip in hand.
He notices SPECK and watches her throw a few rocks.

CALVIN   What are you doing?

SPECK   Throwing rocks.

CALVIN   I can see that.

SPECK   I'm trying to bounce a rock off that piece of wood then hit that can.

CALVIN   Why?

SPECK   It's fun.

> *She resumes her game.*
> *CALVIN considers approaching MISTATIM but can't help watching SPECK.*

You can try if you want.

CALVIN   I'm not really supposed to go to that side of the fence.

SPECK   What's wrong with this side of the fence?

> *She throws it again.*
> *He watches.*
> *He decides to cross the fence.*
> *He finds a rock and tries.*
> *He's way off.*
> *SPECK smirks.*
> *He tries again.*
> *Again, he misses.*

You gotta use just the right amount of force.

> *She tries and succeeds.*

See.

> *As they continue to play, MISTATIM shows interest in their game.*

He gets closer and closer until his head is over the fence just above them.

CALVIN You can only do it because you've been practising.

SPECK Yah. And I'm good at throwing stuff.

CALVIN Can you hit that bottle?

She tries and succeeds.
He tries and succeeds.

SPECK That was easy. Can you reach the puddle?

He tries again and just misses.

BOTH Ohhh.

SPECK Try again.

He tries and just misses.

CALVIN Almost.

SPECK Again.

He tries and succeeds.
They both cheer.
MISTATIM whinnies.
They look up to see MISTATIM's head just above them.

Keep going. He likes it.

CALVIN goes again.

CALVIN   That was my worst.

SPECK   Again.

> *CALVIN keeps throwing rocks.*
> *SPECK reaches up and touches the horse.*
> *She connects with him.*

MISTATIM   Mistatim. Mistatim. Mistatim.

CALVIN   I want a turn.

SPECK   You gotta keep playing.

CALVIN   He's my horse.

SPECK   You gotta keep playing or he'll run.

CALVIN   He's my horse and I want to touch him.

SPECK   Be patient.

CALVIN   I am being patient—I'm letting you touch my horse.

SPECK   Fine then, do it.

CALVIN   Fine. I will.

> *He cautiously reaches up to touch MISTATIM.*
> *MISTATIM pulls back quickly and gallops off.*
> *CALVIN cowers.*

SPECK   You're too scared.

CALVIN   I'm not scared.

SPECK   I know what fear looks like.

CALVIN sees the names on the fence.

CALVIN   What are all these names?

SPECK   It's a record.

CALVIN   Of what?

SPECK   Of everyone who needs to be remembered.

CALVIN   Like who?

SPECK   Like all the people I know who got put in residential schools.

CALVIN   What do you mean?

SPECK   What do you mean what do I mean? Don't you know about residential schools?

CALVIN   A bit.

SPECK   More than a hundred and fifty thousand Indian kids were taken away from their parents and forced to live in awful schools where they couldn't speak their own language or talk about home, where they were starved or beaten or worse and you know "a bit."

CALVIN   I . . . just—

SPECK   That's why I won't go to your school. 'Cause you don't learn anything real. You learn about how to call Indians "Aboriginals," but you don't learn about what happened to my mum and my grandmother and most of the people I know.

CALVIN   Then tell me.

SPECK   So you can call me a liar?

CALVIN   I won't call you a—

SPECK   So you can say it wasn't really that bad?

CALVIN   I won't—

SPECK   This is why I don't talk to rich little white boys like you.

She runs off.

CALVIN   Wait! Speck, wait! Wait!

Lighting shift.

SCENE 5

CALVIN is flooded with memory.
He dreams.
A projection of hands appears behind him:
  • *an adult's hand hangs in a relaxed position*
  • *the child's hand reaches up to take it*
  • *the adult hand pulls away aggressively, or makes a fist*
  • *the sequence replays at different speeds*
CALVIN looks at his hands as the images play and replay.
MISTATIM whinnies loudly as if to wake CALVIN.
Lighting shift.

SCENE 6

Lights up on the fence, which is parallel to the audience with CALVIN's *side downstage.*
MISTATIM *nibbles the grass.*
CALVIN *slowly approaches with a halter.*

CALVIN I'm not scared of you.
I'm not scared of you.
I'm not scared of you.

MISTATIM abruptly crosses to the other side of the stage.
CALVIN *can't help himself from flinching.*
He kicks the fence and sits down.

Fine, but I'm not leaving.

He whistles the tune to a song.
He starts piecing the words to the song.

(sung) Why won't you trust me like I want you to?
Why do you buck when I come close to you?
I'm just tryin' to stop you feeling so blue.
Why won't you trust me like I want you to?

SPECK *appears and watches* CALVIN *sing.*
She sees MISTATIM *likes the song.*

(with more confidence) Why won't you trust me like I want you to?
Why do you buck when I come close to you?
I'm just tryin' to stop you feeling so blue.
Why won't you trust me like I want you to?

SPECK   He likes it.

CALVIN   *(jumping)* Whoa!

SPECK   Sorry.

CALVIN   You shouldn't sneak up on people like that.

SPECK   Is there anything you're not scared of?

CALVIN   I'm not scared of you.

SPECK   You sure?

                    Beat.

                    Did you make that up?

CALVIN   Yah.

SPECK   My kokum would like it.

CALVIN   Your kokum?

SPECK   Yah, my grandmother. My kokum loves country.

CALVIN   You could sing it to her if you want.

SPECK   She'd have to stop crying to hear it.

CALVIN   She cries a lot?

SPECK   Can't stop.

CALVIN   Because of the residential school?

SPECK   *(shrugging)* Maybe. Or maybe 'cause my mum left. Or maybe 'cause she's just sad.

CALVIN   What do you mean?

SPECK   Some people just get stuck in one feeling.

CALVIN   My dad's like that.

SPECK   He's sad?

CALVIN   He's mad.

SPECK   All the time?

CALVIN   Sort of.

SPECK   Even at Christmas?

CALVIN   Even on his birthday. And when he's really mad . . .

SPECK   What do you do?

CALVIN   Try to stay out of his way.

SPECK   Yah.

CALVIN   Yah.

> *MISTATIM brays.*
> *Beat.*

SPECK   Teach me your song.

CALVIN   What?

SPECK   How does it go?

CALVIN   It's not very good.

SPECK   Just do it.

CALVIN   Naw.

SPECK   You scared of that too?

> *Beat.*
> *He starts to teach her line by line and she catches on quickly.*

CALVIN   *(sung)* Why won't you trust me like I want you to?

SPECK   *(sung)* Why won't you trust me like I want you to?

CALVIN   Why do you buck when I come—

SPECK   Why do you buck when I come—

BOTH   —close to you?
I'm just tryin' to stop you feeling so blue.
Why won't you trust me like I want you to?

Why won't you trust me like I want you to?
Why do you buck when I come close to you?
I'm just tryin' to stop you feelin' so blue.
Why won't you trust me like I want you to?

SPECK   We could go racing through the fields
Under a bright blue sky.
Leaping over rivers till it feels like we could fly.

CALVIN   That's why . . .

> *CALVIN starts to line dance. SPECK tries to learn the dance.*

You should just trust me like I want you to.
Just stay calm when I come close to you.
Then you'll see what I know to be true:
You can trust me to be kind to you.

> *CALVIN and SPECK line dance together.*

BOTH   Why won't you trust me like I want you to?
Why do you buck when I come close to you?
I'm just tryin' to stop you feeling so blue.
Why won't you trust me like I want you to?

We could go racing through the fields
Under a bright blue sky.
Leaping over rivers till it feels like we could fly.

That's why . . .

You should just trust me like I want you to.
Just stay calm when I come close to you.
Then you'll see what I know to be true:
You can trust me to be kind to you.

> *The song ends.*

CALVIN   I'm gonna surprise my dad, you know.

SPECK   What do you mean?

CALVIN   With Bruiser.

SPECK   Your dad doesn't know you're trying to train him?

CALVIN   No way!

SPECK   Won't he be mad?

CALVIN   Not when I ride up on him. My dad will be standing in the door of the barn and he'll look at me with disbelief and he'll say, "Cal, what the heck are you doing?" And the anger will drop right off his face and fall to the ground and I'll gallop around the barn and come to a stop and dismount in a cloud of dust.

SPECK   What'll he say?

CALVIN   Nothing. He'll just smile and put his hand on my shoulder and squeeze.

SPECK squeezes his shoulder.

SPECK   Then we'd better get to work.

CALVIN   Yah.

SPECK picks up the halter.

Oh, you mean right now?

SPECK   How do you put this on him?

CALVIN   He goes crazy whenever I try.

SPECK approaches MISTATIM.
She watches him, clicks her tongue and brays, mimicking his behaviour.

Careful, Speck.

> *She rubs the halter on his face to get him used to the fabric.*
> MISTATIM *lets SPECK touch him.*

SPECK   Shhh shhh shhh. Good boy. Good boy.
It's all right, it's okay, shhh shhh shhh.
Shhh shhh shhh.

Okay, I think he's good.
Now put it on him.

CALVIN   Me?

SPECK   I don't know how.

CALVIN   He'll go crazy.

SPECK   Just try.

> CALVIN *approaches and starts to put the halter on.*
> MISTATIM *starts to get worked up.*

CALVIN   I told you, I told you.

SPECK   Shhh, shhhh.

MISTATIM   Mistatim. Mistatim.

SPECK   Shhh, shhh, it's all right, it's okay.

(to CALVIN) Now do it.

> *They put the halter on him.*

CALVIN   That was amazing.

MISTATIM   Mistatim.

CALVIN   How did you do that?

MISTATIM   Mistatim.

SPECK   Did you hear that?

CALVIN   What?

MISTATIM   Mistatim.

SPECK   Mistatim.

MISTATIM   Mistatim.

SPECK   Mistatim.

MISTATIM   Mistatim.

SPECK   Mistatim.
I gotta go.

CALVIN   What?

SPECK   I gotta check something.

CALVIN   But we only just—

SPECK runs off.

Where are you going? Where are you going?

CALVIN looks at MISTATIM.
MISTATIM shakes the halter.
He starts to get agitated.
MISTATIM bucks.
CALVIN runs away.

SCENE 7

MISTATIM is flooded with memory.
He dreams.
A projection of hands appears behind him:
  • *adult hands grip reins*
  • *hands pull violently in all directions*
  • *the sequence replays at different speeds*
MISTATIM looks terrified.

SPECK   Mistatim!

Quick lighting shift.

SCENE 8

The fence has shifted.
The majority of the action happens on CALVIN's side of the fence.
SPECK climbs over the fence into CALVIN's field.

SPECK   Mistatim.

MISTATIM   Mistatim.

SPECK   Mistatim.

MISTATIM   Mistatim.

SPECK   Congratulations, Calvin. You got a Cree horse.

CALVIN   What?

SPECK   Listen. He's sort of . . . talking.

MISTATIM   Mistatim.

CALVIN   Sounds like a whinny to me.

SPECK   He's saying mistatim.

MISTATIM   Mistatim.

CALVIN   Well what does that mean?

SPECK   Horse. Well, technically it means "big dog," but mistatim is the word for horse in Cree.

CALVIN   Really?!

SPECK   It sounded familiar because we learn Cree at school but no one pays attention and we aren't learning about horses but you know the way your mind holds onto things you've heard before and so I crawled into my kokum's bed and whispered "mistatim" in her ear and she looked at me with this look and said, "Why are you talking about horses?"

CALVIN   Wow.

SPECK   Yah.

CALVIN   So . . . you can understand each other?

SPECK   Maybe.

CALVIN   Then say something to him in Cree.

SPECK   In Cree? I'm not very good.

CALVIN   I won't know.

SPECK   He will.

CALVIN   Go on.

> SPECK *pulls a carrot from her pocket.*
> *She offers it to him.*

SPECK   Tansi. *[Hello.]*

> MISTATIM *brays and takes a bite.*

Mistatim, Kimioyo Sin. *[You are a beautiful horse.]*

> MISTATIM *whinnies and takes another bite of carrot.*

CALVIN   What did you say?

SPECK   I told him he's a beautiful horse.

CALVIN   I guess he liked that.

SPECK   Kiya Maskowsiywatim. *[You are a strong horse.]*

MISTATIM whinnies and takes another bite of carrot.

I told him he's strong.

CALVIN   I guess Bruiser likes compliments.

MISTATIM rears at the mention of his name.

What happened?

SPECK   I don't think he likes that name.

CALVIN   Bruiser?

MISTATIM rears.

Okay, okay. Then what should we call him?

SPECK   Tansi ayseekasoyin? *[What is your name?]*

MISTATIM   Mistatim.

SPECK   Mistatim. I think Mistatim is his name.

CALVIN   Tell him we don't want to hurt him. We just want to train him.

SPECK   Namoya Aywiymytootata, Aynotay Nakayita oma. Namoya nantow ci? *[We don't want to hurt you. We want to train you. Is that all right?]*

MISTATIM nods.

Hai, hai. *[Thank you.]*

SPECK attaches a lead to the halter.

Shhh shhh. Ekosi ahnima, Aykaya nantowtayta. *[It's all right. Just stay calm. You're okay.]*
Howe maka aykwa. *[Now come on.]*

> *She makes eye contact with MISTATIM and leads him in a circle around them.*

CALVIN   How are you doing that?

SPECK   I don't know. It's hard to explain.
Takakatim. Kwayskiy Ootaysi. *[Good horse. Other way.]*

> *She clicks her tongue and leads him in the other direction.*

I'm just seeing him.
I'm hearing him.
I'm following him as much as he's following me.

> *She leads him to a trot.*

CALVIN   That's amazing.

SPECK   Whoa . . . whoa . . .

> *MISTATIM stops.*

Takakatim. *[Good horse.]*

(to CALVIN) Your turn.

CALVIN   I don't know . . . I . . .

SPECK   Take the lead.

CALVIN   Maybe you should / keep—

SPECK   You can do it.

       Beat.

Go on.

       CALVIN takes the lead.

CALVIN   Now what?

SPECK   Look at him.

CALVIN   I am.

SPECK   But really see him. Try to feel what he's feeling.

CALVIN   All right.

SPECK   Now tell him which way you want him to go.

CALVIN   This way.

       MISTATIM doesn't move.

It's not working.

SPECK   Try again.

CALVIN   Come on . . .

       MISTATIM doesn't move.

SPECK   Again.

CALVIN   Come on.

> MISTATIM *doesn't move.*

This is never going to work. He won't do what I say because he hates me.

SPECK   He doesn't hate you.

CALVIN   He does. He only remembers that I whipped him and tried to force him to do things he didn't want to do but I didn't know that wasn't right and I'm sorry.

SPECK   Tell him that.

CALVIN   Tell him?

SPECK   Tell Mistatim.

CALVIN   Mistatim. I'm sorry.

> *Beat.*

SPECK   Namoya Oocitow. *[I'm sorry.]*

CALVIN   Namoya Oocitow. *[I'm sorry.]*

> MISTATIM *moves around* CALVIN.

He's doing it! He's doing it!

> *A movement sequence/dance.*
> CALVIN *and* MISTATIM *start working together.*

SPECK watches.
CALVIN leads MISTATIM off.
SPECK finds CALVIN's hat.

SCENE 9

SPECK's side of the fence.
Evening.
It's getting dark.
SPECK is sitting with her back to the fence.
CALVIN enters looking for his hat.
He walks back and forth a couple of times looking, not noticing SPECK.

SPECK   *(holding up the hat)* Looking for this?

He jumps, startled.

CALVIN   You gotta stop doing that.

SPECK   It's too much fun.

She throws him the hat.

CALVIN   Thanks.

Beat.

Did you tell your kokum?

SPECK   What?

CALVIN   How good your Cree was? With Mistatim? And that he—

SPECK   Haven't gone home yet.

CALVIN   Really? Why not?

         She shrugs.

         I'd get in big trouble if I didn't come home for dinner.

SPECK   Guess I'm lucky that way. My kokum doesn't really
         notice.

         Beat.

         (touching the fence) I carved my uncle Floyd's name in the
         fence after he showed me his scars.

CALVIN   *(climbing over the fence)* What scars?

SPECK   On his wrists. A teacher used to tie him to a hot radiator
         whenever he talked Cree.

CALVIN   That's awful.

SPECK   Yup. And it worked. He can't say a word in Cree. *(touch-ing another name)* This is my other kokum. Her name was
         Pauline. She got taken to the school when she was only
         three.

CALVIN   Wow.

SPECK   *(touching another name)* My great aunt Thelma. They
         made her sleep in a bed with a girl who had tuberculosis.
         Thelma caught it of course. And then she died.

CALVIN   Wait, she died at the school?

SPECK   Lots of kids did. *(touching another name)* But they never broke my mum.

CALVIN   What do you mean?

SPECK   She used to talk Cree all the time. At first they cut her hair really short and took away her blankets and made her hold her tongue with her fingers like this.

She shows him.

CALVIN   Ew.

SPECK   But that didn't stop her. Whenever they weren't looking she talked Cree to the other kids—in the bathrooms, on the playground, wherever she could. But then the punishments got worse. One day they caught her talking Cree to this new girl who was crying because she couldn't understand what the teachers were saying. They grabbed my mum and took her to the office where they had these lockers. Like school lockers, you know. And they pushed my mum into one of them and put a lock on the door. She couldn't even sit down and it was dark and really hard to breathe.

They made her stay in that locker all night long and when they finally got her out they made her walk to the dining room where everyone was eating breakfast. They said, "This is what happens to bad girls who don't speak English. And this is what will happen to any of you who talk to this bad girl."

CALVIN   Did she stop speaking Cree?

SPECK   You can't make my mum do anything she doesn't want to
         do. But no one would talk to her after that. At all. And
         the teachers even told other kids to hurt my mum, to spit
         at her and hit her. So that's when she started to run away.
         The punishments for running away were even worse.

CALVIN   Where's your mum now?

SPECK   Don't know. Still running, I bet.

         Beat.

CALVIN   I'm sorry . . . I . . . probably should get home.

SPECK   Okay.

CALVIN   Just . . . my dad, you know?

SPECK   Yah.

CALVIN   See you tomorrow?

SPECK   Uh huh.

         He starts to go.

CALVIN   She probably does notice, you know?

SPECK   Who?

CALVIN   Your kokum. When you don't come home. I bet she's
         wondering where you are right now?

         SPECK stands up.

SPECK   Maybe.
Good night, Calvin.

CALVIN   Good night, Speck.

> *They both exit toward their homes.*

SCENE 10

> *Morning.*
> *Lights snap up.*
> *The fence has shifted places.*
> SPECK's *side is closest to the audience.*
> CALVIN *is with* MISTATIM *calling over the fence.*

CALVIN   Speck! Speck!

(to MISTATIM*)* Don't worry. It's going to be all right.

(calling out) Speck! Speck!

SPECK   I just had the best morning.

CALVIN   Where have you been?

SPECK   With my kokum. When I got home last night she was out of bed and drinking tea and she poured me a cup and we started talking. In Cree. "Weekasin Neetee." *[This is good tea.]* And she was laughing, Calvin, and she had this happy look on her face and then this morning she wanted to garden!

CALVIN   Speck, / I have to—

SPECK   She hasn't gardened for years but we went out front and
started pulling up weeds together—

CALVIN   Speck!

SPECK   You can call me Nitannis now. It means "My Daughter."

CALVIN   Speck!

SPECK   What are you yelling about?

CALVIN   My dad . . . my dad . . . he . . . he . . .

SPECK   Spit it out.

CALVIN   He just stood up at breakfast and said, "That horse has
one last chance." Then he went out to the barn and got
his whip and pulled Mistatim into the ring.

SPECK   What did you do?

CALVIN   I couldn't . . . there wasn't anything I . . .

SPECK   What happened?

CALVIN   He tried to get Mistatim to do things but my dad was
yanking the lead and yelling and cracking the whip and I
could see Mistatim was trying to be calm but . . . but . . .

SPECK   Didn't you say anything? Didn't you tell him?

CALVIN   I couldn't say anything 'cause my dad was backing
Mistatim into a corner and yelling and yanking so
Mistatim reared up and knocked my dad in the head. He

was bleeding and swearing and my mum had to take him to the hospital to get stitches.

SPECK   Is your dad okay?

CALVIN   I think so but . . .

SPECK   But what?

CALVIN   As he left he said he's going to put Mistatim down. He's going to take him to be killed because he's too wild.

SPECK   But he's not wild anymore.

CALVIN   My dad doesn't know that.

SPECK   You've got to tell him.

CALVIN   I can't.

SPECK   You can, you're just scared.

CALVIN   Stop saying that.

SPECK   It's true. You're always scared.

CALVIN   No I'm not!

SPECK   You're scared of me, scared of Mistatim and you're especially scared of your dad. And it hasn't mattered until now. But if you don't tell him what Mistatim is really like, your dad's going to kill him.

CALVIN   I . . . I . . .

SPECK   Fine.

SPECK starts to take the fence apart.

CALVIN   What are you doing?

SPECK   If you won't do something, I will.

CALVIN   What are you doing?
Speck?
Slow down, Speck, wait.
What are you doing?

SPECK   Take this.

She hands him the fence board.

Aykaya nantaw tayta, Mistatim. *[Come on, Mistatim. It's all right.]*
Aykaya nantaw tayta.

SPECK leads a frightened MISTATIM through the fence.

CALVIN   This is crazy . . . this is . . . this is . . .
Speck?

SPECK   Aykaya nantaw tayta, Mistatim.

CALVIN   Please, Speck. Just tell me what you're doing.

SPECK   Aykaya nantaw tayta, Mistatim.

She pats him gently.
She mounts him.

MISTATIM stamps his hooves to become accustomed to the rider.

CALVIN He's never done that before.

SPECK Neither have I.

CALVIN Then how do you know what to do?

SPECK I don't. I'm just doing what feels right.

SPECK rides back and forth on the horse.

Well? Are you coming?

She puts out her hand for CALVIN.
He hesitates then takes her hand and mounts the horse.
They walk.
They trot.
They canter.
They gallop through the fields.

Projection: endless fields and a bright blue sky.

SCENE 11

Thunder clap.
The sky darkens quickly.

SPECK   Faster! Yah!

CALVIN   Wait!

SPECK   Faster! Yah!

CALVIN   It's starting to rain.

SPECK   Faster! Yah!

CALVIN   Where are we going?

SPECK   North.

CALVIN   We have to stop.

SPECK   What?

CALVIN   Stop. Just stop!

> *SPECK brings MISTATIM to a halt.*

SPECK   Whoa, whoa.

> *CALVIN dismounts.*

What are you doing?

CALVIN   We can't just keep running.

SPECK   Once we get to the woods it'll be impossible for them to track us.

CALVIN   The woods are miles away.

SPECK   That's why we gotta keep going.

CALVIN   And then what?

SPECK   And then we'll be free.

CALVIN   But what about food?

SPECK   We'll live off the land.

CALVIN   What about winter?

SPECK   We can survive.

CALVIN   They'll find us, Speck. Sooner or later, they'll find us.

SPECK   What are you saying?

CALVIN   We gotta go back.

SPECK   Go back?! So your dad can slaughter Mistatim?

CALVIN   Of course not, no.

SPECK   Then what?

CALVIN   I'll talk to him.

SPECK   Just like last time?

CALVIN   That was different.

SPECK   How?

CALVIN   I didn't know what to say.

SPECK   Oh, and now you do?

CALVIN   I'll say: "You can't kill him, Dad. You just can't."

SPECK   And he'll say, "I can do whatever I want. He's wild and he's dangerous and he's no good to anyone."

CALVIN   "But he's not wild, Dad, not anymore. Me and my friend Speck, we've been training him. For weeks. And he's good if you listen to him, really, he's so good."

SPECK   "You can't listen to a horse."

CALVIN   "But we do. And he tells us things. Like he doesn't like whips. And he doesn't like yelling or yanking or hitting or being shoved into walls or things being thrown across the room and he doesn't like being called mean names because it makes him mean. And he doesn't want to be mean. He let us ride him, Dad, can you believe it? And I know he hurt you and I hope you're okay but he's really not dangerous. Look at him. Please, Dad. Look at me."

SPECK   Even if you say all that, even if it's true, it won't work on him. Once people shut themselves up in their ways, they don't change—they can't change.

CALVIN   What about you?

SPECK   What about me?

CALVIN   Every part of you wants to keep running right now.

SPECK   What are you talking about?

CALVIN   I can see it in your eyes.

SPECK   You don't know me.

CALVIN   I know you run when you get angry. I know you run when you get sad. I know you run when you get scared and I know you're scared right now.

SPECK   I'm not scared.

CALVIN   I know what fear looks like. I also know you stopped running just now because I asked you to.

SPECK   So what?

CALVIN   People can change.

        Beat.

SPECK   I don't want Mistatim to die.

CALVIN   Neither do I.

        Beat.

This is our best shot. I'm going to do everything I can.

SPECK   How do I know you won't freeze up again?

CALVIN   You don't. You just have to trust me.

She dismounts.

We can ride home together.

SPECK   I can't.
I need to run.

Beat.

CALVIN   Okay.

She runs.

SCENE 12

SPECK *runs, releasing her fear and rage and anger and desire.*
Projection: a horse galloping through fields.

SCENE 13

Lights up on the fence.
SPECK *is carving* MISTATIM'S *name.*
CALVIN *enters.*
SPECK *sees him and continues carving.*

CALVIN   I got grounded.

    Beat.

I thought about sneaking out and leaving a note on the fence or something but I couldn't even get out of the house.

    Beat.

My dad was really mad when I rode up on Mistatim. He said to get inside but I told him everything right there and then. After that he wouldn't talk to me for three days. Then this morning he called me out to the barn. I thought I was going to get it but then he told me he was more scared than he'd ever been when he saw me on Mistatim. I didn't even know my dad got scared.

SPECK   Everyone gets scared.

CALVIN   He told me all the reasons Mistatim was dangerous and I told him all the reasons he wasn't.

SPECK   Good.

CALVIN   He said he's proud of me for standing up for myself, but Mistatim's still dangerous.

SPECK starts to cry.

What's wrong?

SPECK   I didn't even get a chance . . . I didn't even get a chance to say goodbye to him.

MISTATIM whinnies and gallops to the fence.

Mistatim!

She hugs him.

But I don't understand. I thought—

CALVIN   He's on probation. I gotta work with him every day and if I can get him under control, we can keep him.

SPECK   Really?!

CALVIN   Do you think we can do it?

SPECK   We?

CALVIN   You're not going to abandon us now, are you?

SPECK   Your dad won't mind?

CALVIN   I told him I need your help. You're the only one who can really talk to Mistatim.

SPECK   Yah?

CALVIN   I can't speak Cree. Yet.

SPECK   You're a fast learner, neechee *[friend]*.

> *They play tag.*
> *They dance.*
> *They help* MISTATIM *jump the fence.*
> *All exit.*

INSTANT
BY ERIN SHIELDS

ACKNOWLEDGEMENTS

Thank you to Dean Patrick Fleming for inviting me to write this story and directing a beautiful production. Thank you to Mike Payette, Kathryn Westoll and everyone at Geordie Theatre for supporting this play. Thank you to all of the artists involved in the original production for contributing to the development of the script. Thank you to Playwrights' Workshop Montréal and Emma Tibaldo for dramaturgical support, and to actors Mike Hughes, Charlotte Rogers and Jennifer Roberts for workshopping an early draft.

Instant was commissioned by Geordie Theatre in 2015 under Artistic Director Dean Patrick Fleming and produced in 2016 under Artistic Director Mike Payette and Managing Director Kathryn Westoll. It was developed with the support of Playwrights' Workshop Montréal under Artistic and Executive Director Emma Tibaldo.

The Geordie production toured Quebec in 2016/2017 and was presented by Young People's Theatre in Toronto from November 28 to December 15, 2017, with the following cast and crew:

Meredith: Michelle Rambharose
Rosie: Leah Fong
Jay: Dakota Jamal Wellman

Direction: Dean Patrick Fleming
Dramaturgy: Emma Tibaldo
Set and Costume Designer: Cathia Pagotto
Sound and Music Composer: Devon Bate
Lighting Designer: Andrea Lundy
Tour Manager: Mélanie Ermel
Tour Production Manager: Alexandre Michaud
Stage Manager at YPT: Justine Lafrançois
Production Manager at YPT: Amy-Susie Bradford

CHARACTERS

Meredith: fifteen years old, grade ten, passionate about music, wants to be a pop star

Jay: fifteen years old, grade ten, passionate about hockey, wants to get recruited to the QMJHL and eventually play in the NHL

Rosie: fifteen years old, grade ten, trying to help her dad who has multiple sclerosis (MS), quiet, shy, would love to be more popular

SETTING

The play alternates between direct address and naturalistic scenes. The set should be minimal to facilitate quick changes in time and space.

A NOTE ON THE TEXT

There are a few pop culture references and songs throughout the play. Please feel free to make updates to reflect the time and place in which the play is being performed. The same is true of some of the hockey references. In Toronto, we changed the QMJHL to OHL, for example.

Lights up on MEREDITH.
She is fashionably dressed but not a stereotypical "cool girl."
MEREDITH *is confident grade ten student.*
She speaks to the audience.

MEREDITH   I took piano lessons for most of my life but I never really thought about it as something I wanted to do. More like something my dad wanted me to do. He'd be like: "Keep it up, Meredith, you never know when you're going to need a little music in your life." And I'd say, "Fine," but practising was so boring so I kept bugging him to let me stop and finally my mum was like: "If she doesn't want to do it, she doesn't have to do it. She needs to start taking responsibility for her own decisions." And I'm like, "Finally!!!" So my dad let me quit but then one day I'm walking by the living room and I see the piano sitting there with a book open to a Fugue in G minor and my fingers start twitching, and playing on my legs like this, and I can hear this tune in my head like:

(singing) La la la la . . .

So the next day at school, I'm like: "Jay, is this a song:"

(singing) La la la la . . .

Lights up on JAY.

JAY   Yah, the one you just sang.

MEREDITH   No, is it a song you know. Like have you ever heard it before:

(singing) La la la la . . .

JAY   Don't think so.

MEREDITH   And that day I run home from school and go to my piano and this song just, like, flies out of me. And that's when I really start to see it: a crowd of people out there looking up at me and cheering and singing along and I'm just going for it, just losing myself in the words, and for the first time in my whole life I know what I want.

JAY   We were at some winter festival when I was four and I saw all these people whipping by on this outdoor rink. So my mum rents me skates and I'm so excited I can't even sit still for her to lace them up and when I hit the ice I just start to skate. Like I already know how. Like I've done it before. Like a fish can swim or a bird can fly, I can skate, and I'm like: "Look, Mum!" And then I crash into the boards. I've been playing hockey ever since and all I ever want to do is / keep playing.

MEREDITH   Keep playing.

JAY   Head up.

MEREDITH   Head down, listening to the music.

JAY   Listening to the sticks on the ice, to my coach.

MEREDITH   To myself.

JAY   To myself, yah, that's important.

MEREDITH   Right, because it's all in here, it's all inside, except the fans.

JAY   Right, the fans. Watching me.

MEREDITH   Needing me to / play.

JAY   Play hard.

MEREDITH   Work hard.

JAY   Train hard.

MEREDITH   Gotta practise.

JAY   Gotta deliver, but I keep my mind on the dream.

MEREDITH   The dream, yah, the dream. One minute you're dragging yourself from class to class.

JAY   Walking home.

MEREDITH   Eating dinner.

JAY   Yelling at your brother.

MEREDITH   Doing your homework.

JAY   Watching TV.

BOTH   Then BAM!

MEREDITH   You're on a plane to somewhere.

JAY   Because you've been seen.

MEREDITH   Because you've been heard.

JAY   And people know you.

MEREDITH   You're known.

JAY   And people everywhere want a piece of that.

MEREDITH   But you keep it together.

JAY   Keep your head together.

MEREDITH   You still work hard.

JAY   You still play hard.

MEREDITH   But you get to make decisions too.

JAY   Finally.

MEREDITH   About your own life.

JAY   And you can do good things for other people.

MEREDITH   *(to JAY)* That's so you.

JAY   What?

MEREDITH   Thinking about other people even in a dream.

JAY   Whatever.

MEREDITH   Me and Jay have been close for three years.

JAY   Since that science thing.

MEREDITH   You were so funny.

JAY   We got paired up for some science thing.

MEREDITH   Looking at slides through a microscope and we had to draw something—

JAY   A plant cell.

MEREDITH   A plant cell!

JAY   And the teacher kept saying: "That's not what you see."

MEREDITH   But we're like, "Yah that's what we see."

JAY   I mean why would we draw what we don't see when we're supposed to draw what we see.

MEREDITH   Jay was hilarious.

JAY   I'm just like, "What?"

MEREDITH   He starts drawing random shapes and then calls the teacher over and goes: "Is this what I see?"

JAY   Yah, and the teacher's still like: "That's not what you see."

MEREDITH   So Jay's like: "Is this what I see? Is this what I see?"

JAY   Yah.

MEREDITH   And since then, we're close. Well, I mean, we have other friends too.

JAY   A gang of us, yah.

MEREDITH   But girls can be so exhausting.

JAY   Tell me about it!

MEREDITH   *(shoving him)* Jerk! But it's not like we're together.

JAY   No, I mean—

MEREDITH   That would totally ruin it.

JAY   Yah, totally, probably.

MEREDITH   It'd be so weird 'cause we know so much about each other.

JAY   Yah.

MEREDITH   Yah.

JAY   Yah.

Shift.

MEREDITH   Coward.

JAY   I'm not doing it.

MEREDITH   It's funny.

JAY   I don't want to make a video.

MEREDITH   How about I'm like: "What are you looking at, perv?!"
            And you're like: "Why don't you *show* me what I'm look-
            ing at!" And I'm like: "I'll show you this." And then I,
            like, punch you in slow motion and your fake tooth goes
            flying and then you do your goofy smile.

JAY   You mean this one?

            JAY does a goofy smile.

MEREDITH   Other one.

            JAY does the other one.

            Yeahhhh.

JAY   I'm not totally sure how getting drafted works, but I
            think it involves hockey.

MEREDITH   That's why I make videos of every game.

JAY   And I'm cool with you posting a couple of clips from my
            games but this other stuff—

MEREDITH   This other stuff is what gets them to look at the clips of
            your games.

JAY   I don't know, Mer.

MEREDITH   Let's say one of these videos goes viral and some scout
            sees it. He'll be like, "Sorry, honey, I can't go to the
            movies tonight. I gotta go check out Jay James." And
            she's like, "Who?" And he's like, "The kid with the
            tooth." And she's like, "Ohhhh, the kid with the tooth. I
            like him, he's charismatic, put him on the team."

JAY   Or she's like, "Ew, sick, those videos make me barf."

MEREDITH   Come on! Who doesn't like a fake tooth.

> MEREDITH *takes out her phone.*

JAY   Whoa, is that a new phone?

MEREDITH   It's got a better camera.

(into the camera) Hey, everyone, my name is Meredith, and I'm here with *the* Jay James, the most badass hockey player you're ever gonna meet. His nose has been broken three times, he lost his front tooth last year, and if you see him on the ice, you'd better watch your back, because he's 190 pounds of beat-the-crap-outta-you badass.

JAY   Turn it off.

MEREDITH   He laid a kid flat on his back last year.

JAY   That was an accident.

MEREDITH   Gave him a concussion.

JAY   *(grabbing the phone)* Why d'you gotta push it?

MEREDITH   What do you mean?

JAY   I felt really bad about that guy.

MEREDITH   I know, I was only—

JAY   You don't get it—I'm a big guy already.

MEREDITH   So?

JAY   And I'm strong.

MEREDITH   Which is good, right?

JAY   Right, until someone pegs you as a rough guy and they start grooming you.

MEREDITH   For what?

JAY   To be an enforcer, and instead of playing hockey, instead of scoring goals, you end up being sent on to fight the other goon, and I don't want to beat people up.

MEREDITH   Jay—

JAY   I don't want to beat people up!

MEREDITH   Okay, okay. Chill.

JAY   Let's just do *your* video.

MEREDITH   You all right?

JAY   I'm fine. Yah. What do you wanna do?

MEREDITH   Well, I have this idea for a version of "Hello."

JAY   What do you mean?

MEREDITH   We use kitchen stuff for the instruments. Like salt shakers and pots and pans and ketchup bottles so it'd be like: *(singing)* "Hello . . . "

JAY   Wait a second, I thought you were going to sing your own songs.

MEREDITH   Well, yah, but not yet.

JAY   Why not?

MEREDITH   'Cause that's not the way you do it. That's more of a next level kind of thing.

JAY   What?

MEREDITH   Seriously. You gotta build up your subscribers and then take them to the next level so they're like: "Whaaaat?!!! She writes songs too????!!!"

JAY   You just made that up.

MEREDITH   "Whaaaaat?"

JAY   Your songs are awesome.

MEREDITH   And then someone says to someone like Drake: "Look at that kid, isn't she amazing." And Drake's like, "Whaaaat?! I gotta fly that girl to Toronto or Miami or LA or wherever. Gotta get that girl into a studio or be her personal vocal coach on *The Voice*. And my mum's like: "What's the plan here, Meredith. This doesn't seem like a sensible plan." And my dad's like: "Meredith, are you sure this is what you want? This will change your life forever." And it's a hard choice because I love my parents and the cameras get a shot of me with tears streaming down my face saying: "I love you, Mum and Dad, but I know this is the path I'm meant to take." And when I get off the plane there's all these reporters who are trying to get me to reveal my dirty truths, trying to get me to open up about my past, but Drake pushes past them with that weird dance of his and gets me into the limo and takes me to my hotel and I'm like, "Thanks, Drake, I owe you one."

JAY   You're crazy, you know that?

MEREDITH   Whaaaat????

> MEREDITH *turns on the camera.*

Hey, everyone. I'm Meredith and this is my first song on my first YouTube channel. So subscribe if you like what you hear.

> MEREDITH *sings the first line of an Adele song using kitchen utensils as percussion instruments: spoons, blender, pots, pans, etc.*

> *Shift.*

JAY   Forty-seven views.
That's pretty good for a first video.

> *Shift.*

MEREDITH   Here's my second song, guys. Hope you like it.

> MEREDITH *sings the first line of a Justin Bieber song using office supplies as percussion instruments: stapler, scissors, paper clips, etc.*

> *Shift.*

JAY   One hundred and thirteen views.
       You wanna try that song you wrote last week?

Shift.

MEREDITH   Third song, guys, here we go.

> *MEREDITH sings the first line of a Taylor Swift song
> using bathroom supplies as percussion instruments:
> toothbrush, hairbrush, hair dryer, etc.*

Shift.

(to audience) And things were going well. Slow and
steady: more and more likes, more and more views, more
and more subscribers, more and more positive comments
until . . . Rosie.

Lights up on ROSIE.

ROSIE   Hi.

MEREDITH   She's been in my grade since kindergarten but we're not
really close because she's super shy.

ROSIE   I'm not that shy.

MEREDITH   She's like shaking whenever she does presentations.

ROSIE   I just hate presentations.

MEREDITH   She's more of a do-well-on-math-tests kind of girl.

ROSIE   I like math.

MEREDITH   More of a volunteer-to-take-tickets-at-the-dance-so-she-doesn't-have-to-dance-but-can-still-be-involved kind of girl.

ROSIE   It's for student council.

MEREDITH   She's the kind of girl I've known forever, like maybe she was at my birthday party the year we went skating and my mum made me invite all the girls in my class but I don't think she's ever been to a sleepover birthday kind of girl. Totally nice, sure, and she does have friends.

ROSIE   A couple, yah.

MEREDITH   So she's not a total loser.

ROSIE   Thanks.

MEREDITH   She doesn't stand out, is what I'm saying. Doesn't want to stand out until one day she comes out of nowhere and posts this video:

ROSIE   Hi, guys. My name is Rosie. I don't usually do this kind of thing but I really need your help. My dad suffers from MS. MS stands for multiple sclerosis. It means there's damage to the insulating covers of nerve cells in the brain and spinal cord. And that makes it difficult for his brain to communicate with the rest of his body, so he has trouble moving. He has good days, when things seem fine. And bad days when he can't even get out of bed.

MEREDITH   Here's the cheesy part.

ROSIE   But there is hope.

MEREDITH   See.

ROSIE   There's a miracle treatment that's helping people all
over the world, but the Canadian government hasn't
approved it yet. That means for my dad to get treatment
he'd have to pay $50,000. That's why I'm launching a
crowd-funding campaign to—

MEREDITH   She goes on and on like that for a while, and in the background there's this really cheesy music and you don't
quite know what it is until the end of the video when
Rosie starts to sing:

ROSIE   *(singing)* I'll try my best to be your angel
Because you've always been an angel to me.

MEREDITH   And it's then you realize she's singing with herself. Rosie
is harmonizing with a recorded song, which she must
have written because I didn't recognize it.

JAY   It's pretty good.

MEREDITH   I guess her voice is *okay* but the thing that gets people,
the thing that really makes you feel something, is that
she's crying a bit because of her dad.

ROSIE   Sorry, I just . . .

JAY   You really feel for her.

MEREDITH   So this video just takes off.

ROSIE   Eighty-seven views.

MEREDITH   Two thousand three hundred views.

JAY   Five thousand seven hundred views.

MEREDITH   Sixty-seven thousand views. And the comments are like:
"You are the angel. Keep flying."
"Your dad is so lucky to have you."
"I wish I could sing like you."

JAY   She is a pretty good singer though.

MEREDITH   Oh, come on, her voice is, like, cracking.

JAY   'Cause she's upset.

MEREDITH   Yah, I get it.

           Shift.

JAY   What you're doing is really cool, Rosie.

ROSIE   Oh, thanks.

JAY   Are people donating?

ROSIE   I'm getting there.

JAY   You have so many views.

ROSIE   Yah, but just because people watch the video doesn't mean they donate.

JAY   Well let me know if you need any help, or whatever.

ROSIE   Thanks, Jay.

MEREDITH   Didn't know you went for that type of thing.

JAY   What type of thing?

MEREDITH   Mousy, squeaky, needy.

JAY   Don't be a jerk.

MEREDITH   Type of girl you can just tell what to do.

JAY   Stop.

MEREDITH   Type of girl who smiles shyly at hockey games and sips hot cocoa at Starbucks. She probably has a quirky little hobby like crocheting or scrapbooking or writing limericks.

JAY   Yah, well, her brother's on my team so I was just being nice, Meredith. You should try it some time.

MEREDITH   Oh, come on, Jay, her video is soooo cheesy.

JAY   I guess.

MEREDITH   All breathy and wispy and staring deep into the camera: *(singing)* "Pity me, love me, tell me I'm an angel."

JAY   *(laughing)* You're awful.

MEREDITH   That's why you like me.

JAY   Rosie's not trying to be a star or anything, she's just trying to—

MEREDITH   I know, I get why people like it. I just think it's a bit manipulative, that's all.

JAY   Her dad has MS.

MEREDITH A lot of people have MS.

JAY Yah, and she's trying to help.

MEREDITH Well, she has more than 87,000 people out there listening.

JAY And that's amazing, right?

MEREDITH Of course, it's just so much easier to get lots of views if you've got a sick family member.

JAY Meredith!

MEREDITH Sorry.

JAY You're being an asshole.

MEREDITH Yah. I know. Good thing I've got you to keep me in line.

     Beat.

JAY You should really start posting your own songs.

MEREDITH I will. Once something goes viral, I'll—

JAY They're good songs.

MEREDITH Yah, but they're not . . .

JAY What?

MEREDITH The kind of songs people put on YouTube.

JAY What do you mean?

MEREDITH   They're more serious . . . more quiet . . .

JAY   What's wrong with that?

MEREDITH   It's just not the type of thing people are into.

JAY   So I'm not "people"?

MEREDITH   No. You're not.

JAY   Who am I then?

MEREDITH   You're . . . Jay.

> *Beat.*

JAY   *(seeing his mum)* My mum's here.

MEREDITH   Do me a favour and score today.

JAY   Yes, sir!

MEREDITH   I've got videos of a couple of breakaways, but I need a goal.

JAY   Just don't sit near my mum.

MEREDITH   We can always edit out the sound.

> *Shift.*

ROSIE   So I'm at the game with my parents.

MEREDITH   I go in with Jay's mum but tell her I need to film from the other side of the arena and walk away quickly.

ROSIE   Then I notice Jay's mum.

MEREDITH   I notice Rosie. / She's sitting right next to Jay's mum.

ROSIE   We're sitting right next to Jay's mum and she's already
           starting to get worked up.

MEREDITH   "What the heck was that?!"

ROSIE   And my parents are just trying to focus on my brother.

MEREDITH   "Come on, ref!" That's what she's yelling, but then Jay's
           shift ends so she starts to settle down and I decide to
           check my phone.

ROSIE   I check my phone. Just scrolling through Instagram.
           Like like like like like / like like like like like like . . .

MEREDITH   I check my latest video and it's up to 512 views, and I've
           gained a few subscribers, and I take a couple selfies, pick
           the best one, add a filter, post it and wait for people to
           like it or comment.

ROSIE   Then Meredith's photo comes up on my feed. I wouldn't
           usually comment on one of her photos—

MEREDITH   Twenty-three likes.

ROSIE   Like, yes, but not comment because we're not really that
           close so it might be weird.

MEREDITH   Forty-six likes, two comments.

ROSIE   But most people just want lots of comments, and we're at
           the same game doing basically the same thing—

MEREDITH   Fifty-eight likes, five comments.

ROSIE   I just have to think of the right thing to say, just have to dare myself to do it—

MEREDITH   And then I see it. This comment.

BOTH   "You're so pretty. Enjoying the game so far?"

MEREDITH   And I wouldn't normally care who comments but for some reason I'm like, "What?!" We barely know each other and she feels like she can comment on my selfie, on my Instagram and try to what? Try to tell people we're at the same game?

ROSIE   She sees it.

MEREDITH   On purpose!

ROSIE   Is she mad at me?

MEREDITH   I look up and there she is sipping hot chocolate with that mousy grin.

ROSIE   Don't do something stupid, Rosie. Don't do something stupid.

ROSIE waves.

MEREDITH   What the hell was that?

ROSIE   That was stupid.

MEREDITH   Some sort of pretend-shy-nervous kind of wave?

ROSIE   She definitely thinks that was stupid.

MEREDITH   I force myself to smile back. Then I get this feeling. This sick purposeful feeling and as soon as I think it I know I'm going to do it and this calm spreads over me.

ROSIE   Maybe I should delete my comment.

MEREDITH   I log into my fake YouTube account so it'll be anonymous.

ROSIE   Can I delete it?

MEREDITH   I find Rosie's video.

ROSIE   Siri: How do I delete comments on Instagram?

MEREDITH   An ad starts to play because she's up over 100,000.

JAY   Back on the ice. Back in the game. And my mum starts up again. This guy's laying into me, trying to get me going, trying to piss me off.

ROSIE   My dad starts rubbing his eyes.

JAY   He wants to make me drop my gloves.

ROSIE   I ask if he feels dizzy.

JAY   Wants to make me snap.

ROSIE   He says he's okay.

JAY   I've got this under control.

MEREDITH   I scroll through the sucky comments under Rosie's video, wondering if I'll change my mind, if some kind of sympathy will sink in as I look up across the ice at her.

ROSIE   I hope he's okay.

MEREDITH   Nope. I comment on Rosie's video: "Thank God for Auto-Tune."

JAY   He slams into me.

MEREDITH   "What's wrong with you?"

JAY   Yelling and spitting.

MEREDITH   "You suck."

JAY   Trying to make me react.

MEREDITH   "Fat."

JAY   Trying to make me snap.

MEREDITH   "Ugly."

JAY   Trying to make me fight.

MEREDITH   "Fake."

JAY   But my head's in the game.

ROSIE   Jay's about to shoot but gets a stick to the stomach and his mum is yelling beside me: "Gonna call that, ref?!"

JAY   Gotta tune her out.

MEREDITH   "Gonna call that one?!"

JAY   Block out her screaming.

ROSIE   "Wake up, ref!"

JAY   Head in the game.
Gotta stay focused.
Gotta keep going.
Try to get the puck but he's got it
and I'm after him
I'm after him
after the puck down the ice
after the puck behind the net
then he stops quick,
I slam into him,
puck goes flying
and he's pushing me
and yelling things
and spitting in my face
but I got my head in the game
head in the game
head in the game

WHAT'D YOU SAY?!!!
WHAT'D YOU SAY?!!!

MEREDITH   And the whole rink goes crazy so / I look up.

ROSIE   I look up to see / two guys going at it.

MEREDITH   Two guys going at it. / Is that Jay?

ROSIE   Is that Jay?

MEREDITH Sticks are flung.

ROSIE Gloves are dropped.

MEREDITH Helmets go flying and they're both throwing punches.

ROSIE The refs are trying to pull them apart.

MEREDITH But they're really going at it.

ROSIE Punches to the face.

MEREDITH To the stomach.

ROSIE And Jay pulls the guy's sweater up over his head.

MEREDITH So the other guy can't move: he can't punch anymore.

JAY I wanna stop.

ROSIE He's smaller than Jay.

JAY I wanna stop.

MEREDITH But Jay's not letting up.

JAY Wanna stop hitting him again and again 'cause it's past the point, way past the point, but I can't stop can't stop can't stop can't stop until finally I hear my coach saying: "Stop, Jay, stop, come on, you gotta STOP!"

So I do.

And there's this calm.
For a few seconds there's this calm.

Shift.

MEREDITH   You okay?

JAY   I don't know why my mum does that.

MEREDITH   She just gets into it.

JAY   Yah, but it's too much.

MEREDITH   She just—

JAY   It's too much. And everybody sees it. That's why that guy
went after me. Started saying things like: "You chain her
up outside at night? She scare away the raccoons?" I told
her she's gotta calm down, go walk it off in the hall, use
one of her . . . strategies.

MEREDITH   What do you mean?

JAY   Nothing.

MEREDITH   Tell me.

JAY   She's got this anger thing. She'll start by being normal
mad. Frustrated, you know, if she's trying to get us
to clean up or whatever, but if we complain or grum-
ble, even, it's like this switch gets flipped and she goes
crazy mad.

MEREDITH   Like what?

JAY   Like throwing stuff and shoving us and screaming.

MEREDITH   That sucks.

JAY   But she's trying. Really hard. With these books and pod-
casts and I can't tell her not to come to my games. It'd
crush her. I don't know, it's just too much.

MEREDITH   Yah.

Beat.

JAY   My dad used to let me stay up late on game nights. Even
when I was about four or five. He'd explain the replays
and I'd sit still, like really still listening to him and watching him watch the TV. That was the only time he'd talk
to me, and the way he looked at those guys, I remember
thinking, one day, that's gonna be me.

Even now I get this smile on my face thinking about five
years from now when I'm playing for the Habs and my
dad'll turn on the TV—wherever he is—and he'll say,
"Wait a second, that's my kid! That's my kid!" And then
he'll be watching me.

Beat.

MEREDITH   First thing you'll buy?

JAY   I don't wanna do this right now.

MEREDITH   A purple baby grand piano with my name written on the
side. Kind of house?

JAY   Mer—

MEREDITH   Kind of house.

JAY   Triplex.

MEREDITH   Dreaming big!

JAY   One apartment for me, one for my brother and one for my mum so we can stand on our balconies and yell up and down to each other.

MEREDITH   I'm going to get one of those mansions in LA. Not the ridiculously huge ones. A modest eight bedroom. With a pool.

JAY   I'm gonna go crazy on jeans and sneakers.

MEREDITH   Makeup and jewellery.

JAY   Mickey D's.

MEREDITH   Starbucks.

JAY   iPhone.

MEREDITH   iPad.

JAY   Huge TV with Nintendo Switch.

MEREDITH   Good wine.

JAY   Lots of beer.

MEREDITH   Clubs.

JAY   Clubs!

MEREDITH   Every night.

JAY   Every night.

MEREDITH   And we'll pay for our friends.

JAY   Wouldn't be fun without them.

MEREDITH   And they'll be so grateful, like, "Thank you soooo much, you guys are soooo amazing!!!" And we'll be like, "Of course! It wouldn't be fun without you guys and if you had this much money, you'd do the same for us."

JAY   And they'd be like, "Hell yah!!"

MEREDITH   But we'll know that really, most of them wouldn't, which is why it's better us than them.

JAY   I'm going to give money to a hospital.

MEREDITH   I'm going to start a foundation.

JAY   I'm going to create some sort of fund to help kids go to university.

MEREDITH   And I'll buy rink-side tickets to all your games.

JAY   And I'll buy out the first row of all your concerts.

MEREDITH   And it'll be good.

JAY   So good.

MEREDITH   Yah.

JAY   Yah.

Beat.

I got suspended for two games.

MEREDITH   They can't do that.

JAY   Yah they can.

MEREDITH   Can't you talk to your coach?

JAY   It's the league.

MEREDITH   But aren't scouts starting to come?

JAY   Yah, I might miss my chance.

MEREDITH   But there's got to be something you can do?

JAY   I couldn't stop, you know. I couldn't stop hitting him.

MEREDITH   He deserved it.

JAY   Doesn't matter.

MEREDITH   I think it does.

JAY   You shouldn't hurt people on purpose. That's just . . . truth.

Beat.

You seen my mum?

MEREDITH   She had to pick up your brother. She gave me money for an Uber.

JAY   No she didn't.

MEREDITH   Fine, but I've got money.

JAY   I don't want your money.

MEREDITH   I'm taking one with or without you so you may as well catch a ride.

JAY   All right. Thanks.

Shift.

MEREDITH   I felt bad for Jay. Really bad, so I didn't even check up on Rosie's video until I got home that night. I don't know what I expected. Maybe for people to jump on board, write some other mean things ,but most of the comments were attacking me. Well, fake account me, saying I was jealous and stuff like that, then right as I'm looking at it Rosie posts a new video.

ROSIE   *(video)* Hey, guys. I just wanted to say that I know I'm not the best singer in the world. The only reason I posted that video was because my dad is so sick. He nearly passed out at my brother's hockey game today and I'd embarrass myself a million times over if it would mean my dad could walk again.

MEREDITH   I almost threw up in my mouth. And then, of course, she starts singing.

ROSIE   *(singing)* You're the inspiration in my life, you make me carry on.

MEREDITH   And then the gushing starts up again because people get sucked into something like that and ten-year-old girls are writing things like:
"You're just as good as Beyoncé."
"You're so pretty."
"Believe in yourself and you can overcome any obstacle in your path."

ROSIE   It was amazing.

MEREDITH   And it all had this effect on her.

ROSIE   People were so nice.

MEREDITH   She started wearing makeup and doing stuff to her hair.

ROSIE   No one had ever stood up for me like that before.

MEREDITH   She just got more confident or something.

ROSIE   And I'd raised about $18,000.

MEREDITH   They gave her some entrepreneurial prize at school.

ROSIE   My dad couldn't believe it.

MEREDITH   She was even on the radio.

ROSIE   He was happier, too.

MEREDITH   Everyone seemed to be talking about Rosie.

ROSIE   And the strangest thing was that people wanted to hang out with me.

MEREDITH   Well, some people.

ROSIE   Cool people.

MEREDITH   Some cool people.

ROSIE   Asking me to come over after school, eat at their tables in the caf, go outside for a smoke.

MEREDITH   She was everywhere.

ROSIE   I mean, I didn't smoke.

MEREDITH   Just lurking around with my friends.

ROSIE   But it was nice to hang out while other people did.

MEREDITH   And just when I thought it couldn't get any worse.

   Shift.

JAY   What are you doing Saturday?

ROSIE   I don't know.

JAY   You should come to Dave's party.

ROSIE   Really?

MEREDITH   Oh, Jay, come on.

JAY   Why not?

ROSIE   I guess.

JAY   It'll be fun.

MEREDITH   You've got to be kidding me.

ROSIE   All right.

JAY   Great.

MEREDITH   I mean I didn't really care but I get enough of Rosie online and at school and I just needed a bit of a break, and on top of all that:

> *Shift.*
> *MEREDITH is halfway through one of her covers.*
> *She stops in frustration.*

Erg!

JAY   What's wrong?

MEREDITH   It won't work. It's ruined.

JAY   What do you mean?

MEREDITH   I was going to post one anyway, just to prove I—but I can't, I'm too— I can't—erg!

JAY   Meredith?

MEREDITH   My mum says I have to stop posting videos until she gets elected.

JAY   What?

MEREDITH   And after that we'll have a good conversation about the "merits and dangers" of posting videos online.

JAY   You're just singing songs.

MEREDITH   And wasting time. And scaring off future employers. And making myself a target for online predators.

JAY   That's all bullshit.

MEREDITH   The truth is she's afraid I'm going to do something that will embarrass her and then voters will think she's a shitty parent.

JAY   Yah.

MEREDITH   Much better to ignore your kid than let her express herself. Now that's good parenting. And the way she talked about it, like it's just some extra thing I'm doing, like it's not important, like it doesn't really matter.

JAY   What about your dad?

MEREDITH   He likes to "follow her lead" with stuff like this.

JAY   Hey, we don't have to go to the party tonight if you'd rather—

MEREDITH   No, it's good. I need a drink.

   Shift.

   So we're at the party and I'm having an okay time. I'm on my second rum and Coke and talking to people in the hall. I can see Rosie in the living room.

ROSIE I'm doing Jell-O shooters.

MEREDITH It's obvious she never drinks.

ROSIE I don't usually drink but I'm keeping up and hoping nobody notices.

MEREDITH She's had about five already and is giggling uncontrollably.

ROSIE At something Sarah said.

MEREDITH But I'm trying to have a conversation.

ROSIE When someone says something funny, you can't help laughing.

JAY I'm in the kitchen with some guys from my team.

ROSIE And I have to go to the bathroom but I'm holding it in because I don't want to leave this moment, this perfect moment of being with people and listening to people and being heard by people and feeling like I'm one of them but finally I know I have to go. I have to go or I'll pee my pants.

MEREDITH She tries to stand up but falls back down again.

ROSIE We all laugh. It's funny. I'm funny.

MEREDITH She finally gets herself up and makes it over to me and I grab her arm before she falls into the wall.

ROSIE Sorry.

MEREDITH You okay?

ROSIE   I gotta pee.

MEREDITH   There's a line.

ROSIE   Okee dokee.

MEREDITH   And I'm just about to tell her to go home. Just about to
           tell her to get an Uber or something but for some reason,
           instead I say:

           I know you like him.

ROSIE   Who?

MEREDITH   You know who.

ROSIE   Jay?

MEREDITH   I knew it.

ROSIE   Is it that obvious?

MEREDITH   More like pathetic.

ROSIE   Really?

MEREDITH   Kidding.

ROSIE   Oh. Yah. I just thought maybe you guys were—

MEREDITH   Oh, no. No, we're just friends.

ROSIE   He's so nice.

MEREDITH   Yah.

ROSIE And hot.

MEREDITH Yah.

ROSIE And nice.

MEREDITH Yah, you know, Rosie, the best thing to do with Jay is to make a move.

ROSIE What do you mean?

MEREDITH I mean, he's sort of slow when it comes to this kind of thing.

ROSIE You think he likes me?

MEREDITH He did invite you, right?

ROSIE Yah, but that doesn't—

MEREDITH All I'm saying is don't be too subtle.

JAY I'm still in the kitchen.

MEREDITH Just go for it.

ROSIE Right.

MEREDITH That's all I said.

JAY We're laughing about Dave's beer belly.

MEREDITH Just go for it.

ROSIE I still have to pee but I see Jay so I decide to go for it before I lose my nerve.

MEREDITH   She walks into the kitchen.

ROSIE   I'm braver than I usually am.

MEREDITH   Walks right over to Jay.

ROSIE   It's easier to think of things to say.

JAY   I see Rosie coming toward me.

ROSIE   Hey, Jay, what are you drinking?

JAY   She's kinda drunk.

ROSIE   I said, what are you drinking?

JAY   Ah . . . beer.

ROSIE   Is it good?

JAY   Ah . . . yah.

ROSIE   I'm better.

JAY   What?

MEREDITH   Then she gets in close. Starts grabbing at his shirt.

ROSIE   I know you like me.

JAY   Rosie—

MEREDITH   She's got her face really close to his so it's hard to hear what she's saying.

ROSIE   Meredith told me you like me.

JAY   What?

ROSIE   You can kiss me if you want.

MEREDITH   And all the guys in the kitchen start taking out their phones.

JAY   You should go home, Rosie.

ROSIE   Don't you think I'm hot?

MEREDITH   And she starts pulling up her top.

ROSIE   'Cause I'm feeling really hot.

MEREDITH   And the guys are laughing and taking videos.

ROSIE   Come on, Jay.

MEREDITH   She's rubbing up against him.

ROSIE   Don't be shy.

MEREDITH   And Jay looks really uncomfortable.

JAY   Rosie, please.

MEREDITH   Like he doesn't know what to do.

ROSIE   Come on.

MEREDITH   Until finally he says:

JAY   Stop! Rosie, stop!

MEREDITH   And she does.

ROSIE   I suddenly become really aware of everything. Of the disgusted look on Jay's face, of everybody laughing, of all the phones pointed at me, of the fact that I still really have to go pee.

MEREDITH   She starts pushing into people with this wild look in her eye.

JAY   Rosie, wait.

ROSIE   I run to the bathroom, bang on the door, but there's someone inside.

MEREDITH   She's sort of grunting.

ROSIE   I'm trying to keep it in.

JAY   I think she needs to puke.

ROSIE   Just keep it in.

MEREDITH   She's looking for her boots in the pile by the door.

ROSIE   Just keep it in.

JAY   But then Dave comes up to her.

ROSIE   This big guy is standing in front of the door and says:

JAY   "I think you're hot. Wanna kiss me."

MEREDITH   And he opens his arms.

JAY   And he gives her this bear hug and he's joking.

MEREDITH   Yah, he's joking but you can see she wants to get out.

ROSIE   Lemme go.

MEREDITH   But he won't.

ROSIE   Lemme go.

JAY   And I'm like, "Dave, come on!"

MEREDITH   But he's holding her off the ground.

ROSIE   And he smells like sweat and hair gel.

JAY   Come on, Dave.

ROSIE   Lemme go!

JAY   Dave, come on.

MEREDITH   And then I see it.

ROSIE   Oh no.

JAY   We all see it.

ROSIE   God, no.

MEREDITH   It's streaming down her leg.

JAY   Dripping on the floor.

MEREDITH   And there's a puddle underneath her.

JAY   Getting bigger by the second.

MEREDITH   And she lets out this cry.

JAY   Not a loud cry.

MEREDITH   No, it's not that loud, but I hear it.

JAY   So do I.

MEREDITH   Like . . . defeat.

JAY   Dave finally lets her go and realizes what's happened and starts to freak out.

ROSIE   I'm free.

MEREDITH   She's free.

ROSIE   But I can't move.

MEREDITH   She doesn't move.

ROSIE   For an hour, it seems.

MEREDITH   For a minute.

JAY   A few seconds.

MEREDITH   Then she walks out into the night.

JAY   Without her coat.

MEREDITH   I dig through the pile of coats by the door until I find it but by the time I get outside she's gone.

JAY   What did you say to her?

MEREDITH   Nothing.

JAY   What did you say?

MEREDITH   Nothing. Just if she liked you so much she should just go for it.

JAY   Meredith!

MEREDITH   What? I didn't know she'd actually—

JAY   You knew she was wasted, and you knew she'd probably do something embarrassing.

MEREDITH   Why are you putting this on me?

JAY   'Cause you've had it out for her from the beginning.

MEREDITH   What are you talking about?

JAY   I know you're the one who posted those awful things on her video. I know that's your fake account.

MEREDITH   Someone's got to tell the truth.

JAY   Tell the truth about what?

MEREDITH   That she's a terrible singer.

JAY   Even if that was true, why are you going out of your way to say it?

MEREDITH   I thought you were into truth.

JAY   And setting her up to be humiliated.

MEREDITH   Because she's a fake.

JAY   No, Meredith, you're the fake.

MEREDITH   What?

JAY   You say you want to be a singer, to be a real musician, but all you do is post covers of pop songs you don't even like. I mean, what's the point, Meredith?

MEREDITH   I told you, once I get—

JAY   Yah, I know what you say, but that's not the truth.

MEREDITH   Then what is the truth?

JAY   The truth is that you're scared.

MEREDITH   I'm not scared of anything.

JAY   You're scared to put yourself out there.

MEREDITH   And Rosie puts herself out there?

JAY   She goes for what she wants.

MEREDITH   Good to know what appeals to you, Jay. Maybe you should have given her what she wanted in the kitchen.

Beat.

JAY   A scout is coming to my game next Saturday. Please don't come. I need all the focus I can get.

Shift.

MEREDITH   And then he left.

JAY   I left.

MEREDITH   I'd never seen him that mad before.

JAY   But it wasn't an angry mad. More like really really sad.

MEREDITH   Like the way your parents get when you do something wrong.

ROSIE   I got home okay.

MEREDITH   So did I.

JAY   Me too but I couldn't sleep.

MEREDITH   Neither could I.

ROSIE   The videos were already up.

JAY   I didn't look.

MEREDITH   It was all over the Internet.

JAY   I wanted to forget.

ROSIE   Different angles of me pulling up my shirt.

MEREDITH   Like five different versions.

ROSIE   And by the door.

MEREDITH   And in one video I can see myself in the background watching. I'm just watching and I'm . . . I've got this grin on my face.

JAY   I should have done something.

MEREDITH   I'm enjoying it.

ROSIE   I should have left earlier.

MEREDITH   I look at her coat on the chair in my room.

JAY   Hope she's okay.

MEREDITH   I think about messaging her.

ROSIE   There's so many comments.

MEREDITH   It'll blow over.

JAY   Gotta focus on next weekend.

ROSIE   That week was unbearable. It just kept going. Someone took the audio from the video for my dad and played it underneath a video of me at the party. And people said really terrible things. That I was an attention whore. And a slut. And my dad's probably not even sick, and if he is, they hope I have to watch him die and people start asking for their money back and I can't stop looking at it, can't stop reading the comments getting worse and worse and worse.

MEREDITH   I take her coat to the office.

ROSIE   I can't eat.

MEREDITH   The secretary tells me to put it in the lost and found.

ROSIE   I can't sleep.

MEREDITH   I look at the box of grey hats and dirty gym socks and mouldy lunch bags and can't bring myself to put her coat in the box.

ROSIE   Can't go to school.

MEREDITH   I put it in my locker and decide to give it to her when I see her.

ROSIE   Can't leave my room.

MEREDITH   But I don't see her.

ROSIE   My dad asks me what's wrong and I tell him I'm sick.

MEREDITH   I'd give it to Jay but he won't talk to me.

ROSIE   I can't tell him.

MEREDITH   I don't want to leave her coat there over the weekend so I bring it home again.

ROSIE   Can't tell anyone.

MEREDITH   Then it's Saturday night.

JAY   I'm in the locker room.

ROSIE   My parents are at the game.

MEREDITH   My house is so empty it hurts.

ROSIE   I'm home alone.

MEREDITH   My dad's on a business trip and my mum's at some event
and I'm trying to write a new song.

JAY   Trying to focus on the game. I'm taping my stick,
unpacking my gear.

MEREDITH   All that's coming out are songs I've heard before.

JAY   Rosie's brother walks by and shoves me, says, "Move
over, asshole."

MEREDITH   *(singing)* La la la.

JAY   I'm like, "What the hell?!"

MEREDITH   *(singing)* La la la.

JAY   My coach says, "Get it together, Jay."

MEREDITH   I can't concentrate so I go on Instagram and Snapchat
and then I'm watching random videos on YouTube and
decide to check up on Rosie's channel, thinking maybe
she's posted another video or something, but then I see
she's live-streaming. She looks really . . . tired, and she's
holding up this whiteboard that says:

ROSIE   Fifty-nine minutes until the end.

MEREDITH   And I'm like, what? Is she talking about her dad? Then
she rubs out fifty-nine minutes and writes:

ROSIE   Fifty-eight minutes.

MEREDITH   And then she picks up a bottle of prescription pills and
holds it up to the camera.

ROSIE   Fifty-seven minutes till you all get your wish.

MEREDITH   And I'm like, no way, who decides to kill herself over
something like this. We all do stupid shit all the time
and sometimes it ends up on the Internet and you cry
a bit and get over it and then someone else does something stupid so no one cares about your stupid thing
anymore.

ROSIE   Fifty-six minutes till you can watch me die.

MEREDITH   This is ridiculous. She's just doing it for attention, right.
She won't actually do it. Then someone writes: "About
time, loser," and I'm like no no no, this is only going
to get worse. I glance at her coat on the chair looking
deflated and empty. I have to do something.

   Shift.

JAY   You can't be here, Meredith.

MEREDITH   I'm not staying, I—

JAY   I'm on the ice in five minutes.

MEREDITH   I just need to talk to you for a second.

JAY   I gotta focus.

MEREDITH   I know.

JAY   Gotta keep a clear head.

MEREDITH   I know.

JAY   This isn't a game for me, Meredith.

MEREDITH   I know.

JAY   Yah, you do know, which is why you showing up is so—

MEREDITH   Jay, I'm sorry, I just—

JAY   You know my mum works two jobs to pay the rent and put food on the table. You know there's no savings account or university fund waiting in some bank. You know this is it. Hockey is my one shot and if I miss it, there's nothing else. Nothing else for me or my mum or my brother. I'm it. I'm the shot. So if I mess up tonight because I get all worked up over you, I'm screwed.

MEREDITH   You really think I came here to mess you up?

JAY   Not on purpose, but—

MEREDITH   You think I don't know how important this is?

JAY   You do but you're—

MEREDITH   What? What am I?

JAY   You're selfish.

Beat.

MEREDITH   Right . . . yah . . .

JAY   Oh, Mer, I'm just . . . trying so hard.

MEREDITH   Me too.

Beat.

JAY   Please . . . go.

MEREDITH   I will. I'll leave you alone. I just . . . first . . . I need Rosie's address.

JAY   Come on, Meredith, leave the girl alone.

MEREDITH   I'm trying to help.

JAY   You've done enough.

MEREDITH   Believe me, I know.

JAY   Is that her coat?

MEREDITH   Yah, I'm going to give it back.

JAY   You think she wants to see you?

MEREDITH   Just tell me her address.

JAY   Leave it with me.

MEREDITH   I can't.

JAY   Or with her brother, then.

MEREDITH   Will you just tell me where she lives and I'll go.

JAY   Why?

MEREDITH   Her coat . . . I'm going to . . . apologize.

JAY   Don't lie to me.

MEREDITH   It'll be fine.

JAY   What's wrong?

MEREDITH   I can handle it, don't worry.

JAY   Tell me what's going on, Meredith, or honestly I—

MEREDITH   She says she's going to down a bottle of her dad's pills.

JAY   What?!

MEREDITH   She might be faking it but she's doing some sort of
countdown.

What are you doing?

Jay, what are you doing?

No no no, you can't do this.
Her parents are here, I'll go talk to them.
Or her brother.

JAY   No. We let this happen. We fix it.

MEREDITH   Jay. Jay!

       Shift.

JAY   I burst into the night.

MEREDITH   You can't!

JAY   I hear the snow crunch under my boots.

MEREDITH   You can't leave!

JAY   Flip up my hood, hands in my pockets.

MEREDITH   The bus comes right away and I almost don't make it on. Jay paces back and forth. Won't talk to me.

ROSIE   Ten minutes.

JAY   Five stops.

MEREDITH   Maybe we should call 911.

ROSIE   Nine minutes.

JAY   Four stops.

MEREDITH   Maybe we should call her parents.

ROSIE   Eight minutes.

JAY   Three stops.

MEREDITH   Message her, maybe?

ROSIE   Seven minutes.

JAY   Two stops.

MEREDITH   Say something.

ROSIE   Six minutes.

JAY   One stop.

MEREDITH   Jay?

JAY   Off the bus.

MEREDITH   He's running.

JAY   Two blocks, turn right.

MEREDITH   I'm trying to keep up.

JAY   Heart thumping.

MEREDITH   Hands cold.

JAY   Breath sharp.

MEREDITH   Wind fierce.

JAY   Bang on the door.
Ring the bell.
Door unlocked.
Boots off.
Up the stairs.
Into her room.

Rosie?

MEREDITH   And when I finally catch up, finally get to the top of the stairs, I just hear this sobbing. I look in and see Jay with his big arms, his big body, his big heart wrapped around her.

> *MEREDITH closes the laptop.*
> *She puts down* ROSIE's *coat and leaves.*
> *Shift.*

(for YouTube) Okay, everyone, here's something a little different. I wrote this song myself and . . . I don't think I would have the courage to post it if it weren't for a good friend of mine.

Here it goes.

> *MEREDITH sings an original song.*

I'm outta luck,
I'm outta time,
to fix this situation.
'Cause outta fear
and outta shame
and bad communication,
I'm in a sweat,
I'm in a daze,
thinking about you.
So won't you tell me if you're in a state
thinking of me too.

You are the one
who always tells me to stop
whenever I go too far.
You are the one
who picks me up off the floor
and tells me I'm a star.

I'm outta tears,
I'm outta pain,
from this endless separation.
'Cause outta hope
and outta love
and total admiration,
I'm in a sweat,
I'm in a daze,
thinking about you.
So won't you tell me if you're in a state
thinking of me too.

So won't you tell me if you're in a state
thinking of me too.

    Shift.

Hey.

JAY   Oh . . . hey.

MEREDITH   Your mum says you're off to Moncton for the weekend.

JAY   They're flying me out to check out the team.

MEREDITH   Living the dream.

JAY   Something like that.

MEREDITH   Guess the scout came back.

JAY   Yah. Seems like someone made a video of highlights
from all my games and sent it to him anonymously.
And to my coach. And to the coaches of all the Q teams

telling them they shouldn't miss out on the best guy in triple A.

MEREDITH Wow. The person who did that must think you're pretty awesome.

JAY I guess.

MEREDITH I know.

> *Beat.*

I've been helping Rosie with her campaign.

JAY Yah, I was a bit surprised when I saw the video of you guys singing together.

MEREDITH Her family's really nice.

JAY Yah.

MEREDITH And it's a good cause.

JAY Yah.

MEREDITH And Rosie does have a pretty good voice.

JAY Told you.

MEREDITH You were also right about me. I was scared to really put myself out there. Singing covers is different, you know. I can just goof around and if people say I look stupid I can just be like, "Yah . . . so?!" But with my own songs, well, they're important. They mean . . . something, and there's just so much of me in the lyrics, in the music, in the way I sing, and when I perform them I'm not trying to control what I look like or what people are going to think about what I look like. I'm just so . . . myself. I was scared jerks like me might see that vulnerability and purposefully try to ruin it.

JAY So what changed your mind?

MEREDITH You.

      Beat.

JAY It's a great song.

MEREDITH Thanks.

JAY How many views?

MEREDITH Doesn't matter.

JAY I've really missed you.

MEREDITH Yah, me too.

      Shift.

After that, Rosie and I made a few more videos.

JAY We all hung out a couple of times.

ROSIE My brother told my parents what happened.

MEREDITH We raised enough money for her dad.

JAY My team did good but we didn't win.

ROSIE   I talked to a counsellor about it all.

MEREDITH   My mum got elected.

ROSIE   People stopped reposting the video of the party.

JAY   And then it was summer.

MEREDITH   I went to camp.

JAY   I moved to Moncton.

ROSIE   I worked at Dairy Queen and helped out my dad.

JAY   I made it through training.

MEREDITH   I did a canoe trip.

ROSIE   My dad started treatment.

JAY   I got on the team.

MEREDITH   Then, school again.

ROSIE   I joined the choir.

JAY   I boarded with a family.

ROSIE   I made new friends.

JAY   It was a little bit hard.

MEREDITH   I Skyped with Jay almost every night.

JAY   I went to practice.

MEREDITH   I tried out for the musical.

JAY   I went to school.

ROSIE   I got a boyfriend.

MEREDITH   I got a good part.

JAY   I went to practice.

ROSIE   He was awesome.

JAY   I went to games.

MEREDITH   I went to parties.

JAY   I went to practice.

ROSIE   I went out on weekends.

JAY   School, practice, games.

MEREDITH   I loved rehearsals.

JAY   School, practice, games.

ROSIE   I got really into student council.

JAY   School, practice, games.

MEREDITH   I went on a ski trip over the holidays.

ROSIE   I broke up with my boyfriend.

JAY   I missed my mum.

ROSIE   I went to the Valentine's dance with someone else.

JAY   I missed my brother.

MEREDITH   The play sold out.

JAY   I missed Meredith.

MEREDITH   Closing night was the best.

JAY   Wish I coulda been there.

MEREDITH   Awesome cast party.

JAY   Cool.

MEREDITH   How's your nose?

JAY   Sore.

MEREDITH   And your ribs?

JAY   Sore.

MEREDITH   And your spirit?

JAY   Unbreakable.

MEREDITH   That's my guy. You ready for tonight?

JAY   I can't believe we made it to the championship.

MEREDITH   Do me a favour and score tonight.

JAY   You got it, Mer.

Erin Shields is a Montreal-based playwright and actor. She trained as an actor at Rose Bruford College of Speech and Drama in London, England, and then studied English Literature at the University of Toronto. She won the 2011 Governor General's Literary Award for Drama for her play *If We Were Birds*, which premiered at Tarragon Theatre. *If We Were Birds* has been widely produced and translated into French, German, Italian and Albanian. Other theatre credits include *Paradise Lost* (Stratford Festival), *The Lady from the Sea* (Shaw Festival), *The Millennial Malcontent* and *Soliciting Temptation* (Tarragon Theatre), *Beautiful Man* and *Montparnasse* (Groundwater Productions), and *The Angel and the Sparrow* (The Segal Centre).

First edition: November 2018
Printed and bound in Canada by Imprimerie Gauvin, Gatineau

Cover art and design by Meags Fitzgerald

**PLAYWRIGHTS
CANADA PRESS**

202-269 Richmond St. W.
Toronto, ON
M5V 1X1

416.703.0013
info@playwrightscanada.com
www.playwrightscanada.com
@playcanpress